stalked on spring break

emma bray

one

. . .

Riley

I really don't know why I let my roommate talk me into this. Maybe it's because I have nowhere else to spend Spring Break. Granted, I should probably have stayed in the dorm and caught up on some studying. That's why I'm in college anyway. To get my degree to become a social worker.

I really lucked out, all things considered. I was offered a full-ride scholarship based on my high school test scores. And it's a good thing too because with no family to put me through college, I would have had to take out a boatload of student loans to pay my way through otherwise. Actually, I probably wouldn't be here were it not for the scholarship. I don't want to start my life out in debt. I'm pretty sure I wouldn't have done that.

No, I'd probably be working at some dive bar, running myself ragged for tips if I hadn't landed this scholarship.

I remember when my Mrs. Miniver pushed for me to apply. I'd thought it was silly for me to even apply to colleges. But my counselor, bless her heart, had insisted on me applying just to see if I could get in. She filled out some financial aid forms for me, and that's how I ended up where I am now.

I suppose I owe it all to her. She's the closest thing to a mother figure I've had since my mom died.

My heart wrenches within me at the thought. Mom has been dead for five years now, but the thought of her death still hurts.

I think of Mrs. Miniver again. I haven't seen her since I went off to college. Although she was kind to me throughout high school, she has her own family. And it's not like we developed one of those long-term relationships.

I'm just grateful that she took enough of an interest in me back when I was in school to get me on the path I'm on today.

Tears sting my eyes when I think of my mother. I blink furiously to try to hide them, not wanting the other girls to see them and start freaking out asking me why I'm crying when I should be just as happy and excited as they are for our trip.

I think Mom would be proud of what I'm doing. My entire career choice was inspired by her, after all.

If she were still alive, I'd be going home to see her over Spring Break. I'd much rather be doing that than going with a group of girls down to Daytona Beach, Florida. Yeah, I know Spring Break in Daytona is every college student's dream, but I'm just kind of lackluster about it all. I'm mostly only going because my roommate declared it was pathetic for me to stay cooped up in the dorms alone.

Not like she and I are particularly close. I'm not really close with any of my "friends."

I've always been that kind of friend who was a bit of a loner. I can show up and make small talk with the group, but then I can just as easily slip off and do my own thing.

I get along well with all the girls who are going and have never really had frenemies, even if I'm not particularly close to any of them.

We all pile into my roommate's convertible, courtesy of her overly apologetic father. He's always trying to make up for divorcing her mom. Consequently, my roomie always gets anything she wants. Her father's loaded.

I get settled in by the door. Three of us are sitting in the back, and two girls are in the front.

I sit silently as the girls chatter among themselves, making sure that we've got everything.

Suddenly, I feel a prickle at the back of my neck. It runs down my spine and has my heart speeding up and my breath catching.

I turn to look around me. I shake my head at my paranoia when I find nothing there.

This is totally bizarre. Ever since about a week ago, I've been feeling like someone is watching me, which is crazy because who would be watching me? I don't really have any enemies, and I don't really know anyone. It's just me, myself, and I.

It's been that way for five years now…

Maybe I'm just so used to being alone that I'm starting to get paranoid.

I chew on my lip as my eyes continue to scan our surroundings. Still, I think it's weird that I suddenly started feeling these little pinpricks running up and down my spine about a week ago.

I take a deep breath and tell myself to settle down, that I'm just being silly.

Maybe I'm just super stressed out with my course load. Maybe my roommate is right. Maybe I need to get away, soak up some sun and relax. I'm just stressing myself out too much with my studies. That's all.

Casey throws her hands in the air where she's sitting in the passenger seat and lets out a loud "Whoo!"

She turns up the music, and we start speeding off down the highway with the top down. Our hair whips out behind us, and I can't help the grin that overtakes my face.

I have to admit this does feel good.

Maybe my roomie is right.

Maybe all I need is to loosen up a little.

I tilt my face up, basking in the feeling of the warm wind grabbing my hair and whipping it back off my face.

This feels good.

———

Parker

I'm following behind the convertible filled with coeds. I make sure that my nondescript SUV is a discreet distance away from them so as not to draw any attention.

Riley already senses me. I see it in the way she glances over her shoulder when my eyes are on her, the way her eyes flit all around as if she's looking for the source of the shivers running up and down her spine.

I don't like the thought that I'm scaring her or making her paranoid, but knowing that she *feels* me gives me a sense of satisfaction.

A week. I've been out for a week.

Theoretically, I could get close enough to touch her, to talk to her.

Yet I don't.

Not yet.

I frown when I see the girl in the front passenger seat throwing her hands up in the air as they go speeding down the highway.

She's drawing attention to them, and every man in the vicinity is slowing down to look over at all the cute babes in the car.

That one in the front passenger seat…out of all of Riley's friends, I dislike that one the most. She's trouble. Wild and uninhibited. I already know she's the one I'm going to have to worry about getting my innocent little Riley in trouble.

Spring Break. I grimace at just the thought of it. I never went to college, but I remember very well what Spring Break entails. Hey, just because you don't go to college doesn't mean you can't show up.

Spring Break. Too much alcohol, *Girls Gone Wild*, and horny dudes just waiting to take advantage of them.

My lips press into a thin line. Nope. Not going to happen on my watch.

The hardest part about being locked up wasn't the lack of freedom. It was being unable to protect Riley. I know very well how dangerous this world can be for a young woman on her own.

Protecting her is what got me locked up in the first place.

Do I regret it? Hell no.

Would I do it again? In a heartbeat.

I'd give up anything if it meant I could keep Riley safe.

Riley. The girl who changed my world with just one smile.

I still remember that moment clear as day. I'd had a pretty rough trip. I'd just gotten back on the docks. Work on the barges is no picnic. It's tough physical labor and long hours at sea.

But the pay is good. And if you're a loner and don't have a family or anything—like me—then it's suitable. It's grueling work and kept me busy.

Still, that doesn't mean a man doesn't get down from time to time, and I'd been feeling pretty low.

I'd been walking along, minding my own business, when this little fairy came flying by. She'd had her nose in a book and hadn't been paying a bit of attention to where she was going.

She bumped right into me. It wasn't more than the slightest jostle, but it was enough to grab her attention. She clutched the book to her chest and turned bright blue eyes up at me.

"Sorry!" she apologized swiftly before gracing me with the most beautiful smile I've ever seen in my entire life.

It reached her eyes and shined brighter than her golden blond hair. She looked like an angel standing on that street. All innocence and purity and light.

My chest squeezed painfully. "It's okay," I finally managed to mutter gruffly, but she was already flitting away like a little butterfly.

Panic had gripped me at the thought of never seeing that smile again. So I'd followed her.

And I've been following her ever since.

Well, until I got locked up.

But I'm out now.

I just thank whatever deity is out there that she wasn't harmed while I was locked away.

No one is ever going to crush my little butterfly. Not while I'm alive.

I'm sure she doesn't remember me. Why would she? I'm a nobody to her. Just some random stranger she bumped into on the street. Another face in a sea of many.

She has no idea that her innocent actions changed my life that day.

I followed her for weeks, learning everything I could about her. She was only eighteen back then and was waitressing at a bar down near the docks. It was summer, and she was set to start college in the fall.

While I was proud at the thought that she was smart enough to get into college on a full ride scholarship, my chest tightened every time I thought of her being on a campus with all the young men who would undoubtedly be there.

I'm ten years older than her. Some would say that's too old for her. That she's too young for me.

But I don't care about her age. The longer I watched her, the more convinced I became that she's mine.

I didn't know how I was going to approach her, but I knew I couldn't let her go off to college without at least introducing myself into her life.

Before I could do that, though, fate intervened.

I didn't like where she worked. There were too many men who went in there just to stare at the pretty waitresses. And Riley was by far the prettiest.

A pair of dudes who I instantly knew were up to no good went in and tried to get too handsy with her. Fortunately, the manager threw them out before I lost my temper and barged in to take care of it myself.

However, while they were outside grumbling, I

heard them plotting their revenge. They planned on waiting until my girl got off work and dragging her into the alley out back to "teach her a lesson."

My vision went red with rage at just the thought of it.

Suffice it to say, they never got the chance to enact their vengeance. I came back to my senses just in time to keep myself from beating them completely to death. Unfortunately, a camera caught my actions on videotape, and I was sentenced to prison. I got out in two years on good behavior.

Ironic that I'm the one who went to jail when, if I hadn't done what I'd done, they'd have most definitely assaulted and maybe even killed a woman. My hands tighten on the steering wheel just at the thought of it, and I take in several deep breaths to calm the murderous rage that threatens to overtake me.

Their actions were the ones that were premeditated —not mine.

Of course, I didn't even try explaining that to the DA. I already knew none of my excuses would matter. No, I just squared my jaw, manned up, and did my time, intent on doing the best I could to get home to Riley as quickly as possible.

I stayed away from all the prison drama and made it clear no one was to mess with me.

I thought of her every day I was locked away,

constantly restless, needing to get out and make sure that nothing like what those men had planned ever happened to her.

She's such an innocent, fragile, delicate little thing. Completely unaware of the danger she'd been in.

I've been pleased with what I've observed since I've gotten out of the pen. Riley is a good girl. For the most part, she leads a quiet life.

But this Spring Break trip has me feeling all sorts of anxiety. I wish I could just stop her from going.

But since I can't, she won't be going alone.

I'll be there to watch over her and keep her safe.

It's my most important mission in life.

two

. . .

Riley

The Atlantic Ocean is beautiful. I ditched the lounge chair about an hour ago so I could lie directly on the sand. I love the feeling of the sand gliding through my toes.

I listen to the gentle roar of the waves crashing on the shore. It's like a peaceful lullaby. Gosh, I can't imagine how amazing it would be to go to sleep and hear that every night.

Of course, my lullaby is interrupted by the sounds of loud music, laughter, and partying from all the Spring Breakers here on the main strip. I honestly wish

I could find a quieter and more secluded part of the beach to just soak up nature at its finest.

I apply more sunscreen to my skin. While I might be wearing an itty bitty, teeny weeny, yellow bikini, it doesn't have any polka dots on it. And my skin is so fair I've made sure to reapply protection every two hours religiously because I certainly don't want to be getting sunburned and ruining the rest of my vacation.

I'm sure my skin can tan, but I just didn't obsess over that like the other girls did. For a month before we came down here, they all lay in tanning beds to make sure that they were already tan for our trip.

I didn't do that, though. There's no way you'd ever get me in one of those things. Not only am I too wary about their harmful UV rays that can cause skin cancer, but I'm also way too claustrophobic for that.

Hey, I saw *Final Destination*. I saw how those girls died in that tanning bed.

Nope. No way. I'm not taking any chances.

I hear a bunch of hooting and hollering and look over to see the crowd that has formed around the girls entering the wet T-shirt contest.

I wrinkle up my nose. No way I'd ever do that either. I'm not a prude or anything, but I don't want all that attention on my body.

I don't have the assets for a wet T-shirt contest,

anyway, not with my little breasts that are barely a B-cup on a good day.

And I might have blond hair, but I'd certainly never call myself a blond bombshell.

I'm short and tiny. I always have been. I was always the shortest kid in my class growing up, which meant that when the teacher made us form a line from shortest to tallest, I was always at the very front of the line. I smile at the memory. I guess being short does have its perks—at least it did back in grade school.

It's nearly noon, and the sun is getting brutal. I twist my hair up into a messy bun before I go to dip my overheated body into the water.

The water that tickles my feet is so warm, it's like bath water, but after I get my entire body wet, the breeze that kisses my wet skin feels so refreshing.

I'm standing in up to my hips, letting the waves crash around me when I feel it. That little prickle at the nape of my neck.

I turn around, my eyes scanning the beach. I already know I'm being completely ridiculous, though.

There are hundreds of people on this beach. I mean, it's completely wrapped up for Spring Break, so of course there are eyes on me. Me and every other warm-blooded female here.

Everyone's checking each other out. So why should

I feel that ominous little pinprick at the back of my neck like I'm being watched?

I'm obviously paranoid, and I have no idea why.

Still, I can't shake the feeling that there's a *certain* pair of eyes watching me. I don't know who they belong to, but I get the feeling that I'm being followed.

I'm broken from my paranoid reverie when the girls suddenly run up to me and start pulling me along with them to join their volleyball team.

I'm not an athletic girl at all. I totally suck at sports, but I need something to take my mind off of my paranoia, so I let them lead the way.

Get a grip, Riley, I mentally tell myself. *You're on Spring Break and surrounded by tons of other college students. Nothing's going to happen to you out in the open like this.*

Why don't I believe myself?

———

Parker

She's looking too perfect in that little yellow bikini. My Riley might not be a very tall or curvy girl, but she's got just enough curves in all the right places to whet a man's appetite.

I don't like the way all these fuckers are staring at

her either. I glare at more than one of them, but the sad truth of the matter is I can't keep all the eyes on the beach off my girl. Not when I can't just walk over there and wrap my arms around her, staking my claim.

No matter how tempted I may be to do just that, I'd surely frightened her to death. Still, it's hard to suppress the urge to go and cover her with my shirt.

I can't help scowling as I watch her prance around in that damn bikini that's more revealing than a bra and panties.

Why can't she at least put her little dress back on? She's killing me here. I know I'm probably biased, but Riley is the most beautiful girl on this beach, and I can't stand knowing that she's treating every jerk-off here to the sight of her beautiful little body that should be all for me.

I watch her surreptitiously out of the corner of my eye. I've got shades on, of course, but I refrain from staring directly at her.

To her, I'm just another guy on the beach. I'm taking care not to draw any attention to myself, though when her giggles flow over to me sounding more melodious than the sweetest symphony, it's hard not to stare—especially when this prick steps up beside her and takes it upon himself to start leading her through the motions of how to serve the volleyball.

My hands clench into fists at the sight of another man's fingers on her skin.

I'm about to say fuck it and completely blow my cover when Riley wisely steps away from him, giving him a tight smile.

I relax at the evidence that she's not into him.

She throws the ball over to her friends and then makes some excuses before she's out.

Good girl.

I relax even further when she returns to her spot on the beach and lies in the sand.

That's good. If she's going to be here on Spring Break, I'd much rather have her sitting by herself rather than playing and partying with all these idiots that only have one thing on their minds.

She stares out over the ocean serenely. She looks so pretty and peaceful. I wish I could join her.

One day, I tell myself. One day she and I will sit on the beach together, and it'll be perfect.

For now, I content myself with watching her soak up the sun while I soak up her.

three

. . .

Riley

"I don't know," I tell the girls.

Casey scoffs and rolls her eyes. "Come on, Riley. We didn't bring you all the way down here for you to stay holed up in the hotel room every night. You're coming to the bonfire with us tonight." Her voice brooks no argument.

I like sitting out on the beach during the daytime. It's so relaxing to stay there and soak up the sun, and since I've been doing such a good job of keeping sunscreen on my skin, I've actually started to develop a bit of a tan without burning.

Despite the little prickles that I keep feeling at the

back of my neck, I'm actually enjoying myself and relaxing. Isn't that what this whole trip is supposed to be about anyway?

Well, that's what I was told, but I'm quickly starting to see that for my girlfriends, it's really all about partying.

That's just not my scene and never has been. They've been hitting up clubs every night so far. And I've stayed back in the room because clubbing just so isn't my vibe. I'm too introverted and awkward for all that. Besides, when all the girls are gone, I can sit on the balcony, listen to the roaring of the waves, and look at the moon as it shines down over the ocean.

That's what I like. Those simple little things.

But it's clear Casey is having none of my excuses tonight. She's already dragging me over by the hand, and the other girls are pulling clothes out for me to wear. One of them is already running her fingers through my hair while yet another one is getting out her huge makeup box.

I sigh. It looks like this is happening whether I want it to or not.

And honestly, the girls were nice to even invite me. I should be glad they want to include me in their festivities. At least I'm not shunned or anything.

I don't want to look like a spoilsport by not

agreeing to at least spend one night with them, so I let them doll me up.

When they stand me in front of the full-length mirror with wide grins on all their faces, I gape at my reflection.

They've got me in a tube top and a mini skirt. My hair is left loose to flow down to my waist. Bree somehow managed to curl it into soft waves that are just so beachy and perfect. My makeup isn't overdone, yet the smoky eye definitely brings out my blue orbs.

I actually feel very pretty.

"Wow, you guys," I breathe.

"You're welcome," one of the girls says.

"Yeah, you look totally hot," Casey agrees, nodding her head approvingly before she grabs my hand and starts pulling me toward the door. "Okay, let's go."

While I definitely felt like my reflection was way prettier than usual when we were back in the hotel room, once we step out onto the crowded beach, I quickly realize that I don't have the confidence to pull off this look.

There are too many pairs of eyes on my naked skin. And that's totally crazy, right? Because I've been parading around the beach every day in my barely-there bikini. I know that I'm technically more dressed than I am when I'm in my bathing suit, yet somehow, I feel more exposed in this tube top and miniskirt.

We join a group of guys that the girls obviously know, and I'm introduced to everyone.

"Hey." I wave awkwardly like the total dork I am. Nobody pays me any mind, though. They all pair off until one guy and I are left standing next to each other.

He's smiling down at me, and I give him a nervous smile back.

"Drink?" he asks me, handing me a Solo cup filled with some sort of pink-looking liquid.

"Actually, I'm not much of a drinker…" I begin, but he cuts me off.

"You can't even really taste the alcohol in it. It's really good. Girls love it." He flashes his smile at me, and a lock of his blond hair falls over his forehead.

Okay then.

He's attractive and seems nice enough, and since the girls have just left me here with him, I accept the cup and take a tiny sip, not wanting to seem difficult or stand out even more than I probably already do.

My eyes widen in surprise. He's right. It's actually really tasty. It's light and fruity and sweet. I take another sip.

"Good?" He raises his eyebrows at me.

"Yeah," I agree. He cracks another grin then and reaches out and takes my hand. He begins walking us along the shoreline away from the bonfire.

I glance back behind us. "Aren't we going to join the others?"

He smiles down at me again. "I thought we could take a walk, just you and me. Get to know one another a little better."

I glance back behind us once again, taking in the dance party that has already erupted around the bonfire. Girls are twerking, and guys are hooting and laughing as they watch them.

Yeah, that's totally not my scene.

"Okay," I agree.

I don't remember the guy's name, but I don't know how to ask him without seeming like a total idiot since we were literally just introduced to each other less than five minutes ago. I was so overwhelmed, I didn't really pay attention.

Fortunately, I don't really have to say much. He pretty much carries the whole conversation, only stopping every now and then to ask a few questions about where I'm from and what I do, what I'm majoring in.

Then he goes right back to talking about himself.

I'm barely paying attention to him as I sip my drink and keep casting glances out over the ocean.

I can't seem to get enough of staring at the water. I don't know how long we've been walking, but I suddenly notice that I'm starting to feel tired. My limbs feel heavy, and the waves seem to be melding together with the sky.

I blink a couple of times to try to clear my vision. I glance back behind us and notice that I can't see anyone. In fact, I can barely see the light of the bonfire from here.

"I think we should go back," I say, but my words sound unnatural and slurred. My tongue feels thick, and it takes a great effort for me to get the words out.

I manage to look up at him, and I see his mouth moving, but the words meld together unintelligibly.

I'm focused on his lips, trying to make out what he's saying when everything finally blurs together completely.

And then *nothing*.

———

Parker

Damn it! I knew I should have intervened before now. When I see Riley's body start to slump, I somehow move with superhuman speed to jerk her from the prick's arms before landing a solid punch to his face, instantly knocking him out.

Once the asshat thumps to the ground, I pay him no mind. He'll be out for a little while now.

I turn to my little Riley and stroke her blond hair out of her face. I'm vibrating with fury at the knowledge that he drugged her, beating myself up for not seeing it sooner. At the same time, I can't help noticing how tiny and fragile she feels in my arms, how silken her long hair is as it brushes over my skin.

All the times I imagined holding her for the first time, it wasn't like this.

I glare down at the comatose body. My fingers itch to make him pay for what he's done, but getting Riley to safety is a more paramount concern.

I can't be entirely sure what he drugged her with, but if I had to take a guess, I'd go with Rohypnol.

My jaw is clenched tightly as I try to stem the murderous rage coursing through my veins like hot fire. That prick doesn't know it, but he's just sealed his fate. No one hurts my little angel and gets away with it. He'll get what's coming to him sooner or later. Make no mistake of that.

I carry Riley back to my hotel room where I can keep an eye on her and make sure she withdraws from the drug safely.

Although she's dead weight in my arms, she's still as light as a feather, and I can't help marveling at her.

Her skin is a light bronze now. She's always been fair, and while I love her fair skin, she seems to have a

healthy glow about her now. Her light tan comple-
ments her blond hair.

I leave her fully dressed, only removing her sandals
before covering her up in my bed. My hand skims over
the toned skin of her stomach before I stop myself.

I refuse to feel her up while she's passed out. Doing
that would make me no better than the asshole who
drugged her, and that thought sickens me.

No, when I touch Riley for the first time, I want her
to be totally lucid and aware of my touch.

I allow myself one last touch, just to stroke the hair
back from her face, before I force myself to pull up a
chair and sit guard beside the bed.

It looks like my little angel and I will be meeting
soon.

four

· · ·

Riley

I awaken slowly, blinking my eyes to clear the blur all around me. When I try to sit up, it feels like I've been hit in the head with a baseball bat. I feel so heavy and can't help the groan of discomfort that passes my chest.

"Easy there, little bird." A low, husky, masculine voice speaks. A pair of strong hands help me sit up, propping pillows behind me before leaning me gently back against them.

Once, I'm settled, a water bottle is shoved into my hand, and I gratefully take a long drink, my throat parched. The refreshing water trickles down it soothingly.

My eyes widen as I take in the lavish room that's obviously *not* the one I've been staying in with the girls.

What happened last night? My mind casts about. The last thing I remember is walking along the beach with a guy, and then nothing.

Fear grips me as I realize there's only one of two explanations for this. One, all that alcohol must have gone to my head, and I blacked out. Or two, I was drugged. Seeing as how I didn't even finish the whole cup of what I was drinking, I'm willing to bet it's the second option.

My eyes flick up to the man towering over me, and I swallow as I'm hit with gunmetal gray eyes. His hair is dark, and there's a shadow of dark stubble lining his jaw. He's wearing a white T-shirt that clings to every muscle of a *very* defined chest. He's obviously older than me, though he's definitely still young. I wouldn't put him anywhere past early thirties at the most. But he's such a *man*. Experience and self-assurance surrounds him.

Despite the white he's wearing, he still seems to be shadowed in darkness.

Everything about him is just dark and powerful.

Beautiful.

My cheeks heat when I realize I'm gaping at him

open-mouthed, and he's just standing there stoically, watching me.

"You're not..." I trail off as I realize I don't even remember the guy's name from last night.

The man's eyes darken, and his lips press into a thin line.

I swallow again nervously and change tactics. "Who are you? How did I get here?"

His eyes never leave mine as he answers, "I'm Parker. I found you passed out on the beach last night. Suspected you might have been drugged, so I brought you here to sleep it off."

He found me on the beach? Does that mean whoever I was with had just left me lying there all alone? What happened?

I become more aware of my body. Surely, I didn't lose my virginity last night because I feel the same as always. Aren't you supposed to be sore after your first time?

I pull down the covers and look at my body, relief surging through me to see I'm still dressed. I blush when I remember what I'm wearing, though. Well, *dressed* is a relative term, I suppose.

I look up to see his thoughts mirroring my own, and my skin only becomes more heated with embarrassment as I pull the covers back up.

"Nothing happened. I swear." His eyes capture

mine, his mouth grim. I see the truth in them, and I nod. I believe him.

"I'm Riley," I finally introduce myself to him. He doesn't react. He just keeps staring down at me with those intense gray eyes of his.

"Well, thank you," I tell him sincerely. I pick at the cover, unable to meet his eyes as I ask the question that's burning at me. "Was I, um—" I falter, unable to voice the words.

His voice is soft as he reassures me, "Nothing happened to you. I made sure of that."

I peek a glance up at him, surprised at the steel lining his voice at that last statement.

"You rescued me?"

He doesn't answer. He just continues staring down at me.

So he didn't exactly just *find* me on the beach. Did he see the guy trying to assault me? I shudder thinking of what might have happened if he hadn't shown up when he did.

I push the covers off me and swing my legs off the side of the bed. "I need to be getting back. The girls are probably worried about me."

I make a valiant effort to stand, but as soon as my feet hit the floor, everything starts spinning again. I start going down, but strong arms catch me and ease me back down onto the bed.

"Easy there, little bird." He repeats that same phrase again, his voice gentle and his brow furrowed with concern. "Why don't you stay here and rest a while longer?" He digs into his pocket and pulls out his phone. "Use my phone to call your friends if you want and let them know you're okay."

I reluctantly sag back down into the comfort of his hotel bed, which is way more luxurious than the one I share with the girls. Then I accept his phone with a grateful smile and dial my roommate. She doesn't answer, but I leave her a voicemail telling her that I met someone and I'm okay.

It's not totally a lie. I'm just not about to let the other girls know about my nearly catastrophic night. I don't need them thinking I'm even more of a baby or loser than I already am.

And I did meet someone, just not in the way my voicemail implies.

"I'm sorry," I apologize to Parker as I hand his phone back to him.

The furrow in his brow deepens. "For what?"

I bite my lip and shrug. "For crashing your place. I'll be out of your hair soon. I promise." I let out an awkward laugh, trying to make light of the situation, but that only seems to cause him to frown more.

The bed dips slightly as he sits on the edge of it. He

doesn't touch me, but I can feel his body heat burning me through the covers.

"Don't ever apologize for the actions of someone else." His eyes burn into me with intensity. "And you're not bothering me, little bird. I promise. You're more than welcome to stay as long as you need to."

He raises his hand like he might reach out and stroke my face, but it just hovers there between us for a moment before he pulls it back and stands, running it through his dark hair.

I let out a breath I didn't realize I was holding, simultaneously and confusingly relieved and disappointed.

"Let me go grab you something to eat before the breakfast bar closes. I'll be right back." He takes off toward the door but stops midway there and looks back at me.

"Don't try to get up on your own," he warns me sternly. "You're still weak, and we don't want you falling and hitting your head or something. I'll be gone ten minutes tops."

With that, the door clicks shut, and I'm left lying there in his bed trying to process everything—most importantly my dark savior and why he seems to care so much.

———

Parker

What is wrong with me?

It's true that I left to go get my little angel some food, but I also had to get out of there to keep myself from touching her. She was nearly assaulted just last night, and all I can think about is putting my hands on her skin.

She doesn't know me, and she's probably scared out of her wits. She's not ready for anything like that.

I take in a deep breath. I've got to get myself under control. But it's hard. It's hard being this close to her and not claiming her completely in every way.

Every atom in my body is screaming for me to do so.

She looks so beautiful and innocent and sweet. She's so tiny that all my protective instincts surge to the surface.

I pile a plate full of all the fresh fruits that I know she loves. I add a few carbs and proteins on there as well because I'm going to try to get her to eat something more substantial. But I already know after watching her for so long what she favors.

I grab a glass of orange juice and some milk for good measure too. Some nourishment will go a long way toward making her feel better.

My heart wrenches within me at the thought of

letting her go back to those so called "friends" of hers. The ones who left her all alone with that prick who ended up trying to take advantage of her. I hate to have to be the one to break this to her, but her friends aren't such good friends. I want to wring every one of their skinny little necks for putting my angel in danger like that.

If I had to bet money on it, I would bet that that trouble-making one—Casey, wasn't that her name?—probably bullied my sweet Riley into going out with them.

She's been a good girl every night, staying in by herself, sitting on the balcony where I could watch her.

But then last night, I about shit myself when I saw her walk out of their room dressed in the skimpiest little outfit I've ever seen her in.

I know damn well those weren't her clothes.

And I know those motherfucking friends of hers are the ones who had her all dolled up like that It took more control than I thought I possessed to keep from storming over there and flinging her over my shoulder right then and there. I wanted so badly to cover her up and take her home with me.

No one should see her looking like that. No one except me.

She's mine.

I haul my offerings back up to my room, and it's

like a punch in the gut to see her sitting propped up in my bed like she's waiting for me. I can almost imagine that she acknowledges she's my girl and that we just spent a wild, passionate night in bed and she's just been lounging around, waiting on her man to go bring up some food to feed her before we spend the rest of the day getting lost in each other.

Soon, I tell myself.

I set the plate and drinks on the table before I go to the bed to help her. She's stubbornly independent, though, and gets up on her own while I hover nearby so I'll be there to catch her if she falls.

While my chest swells with pride at the sight of her persevering on her own, I also ache to curl her into my arms. I would have just carried her over to the chair if she'd let me.

Her eyes widen, and she lets out a little laugh when she sits at the table. "There's no way I'm going to be able to eat all of this." She stares down at the over-flowing plate.

I shrug. "Eat as much as you want. The more you eat, the faster the hangover will go away though," I try to advise her.

She shakes her head and gestures to the seat across from her. "Why don't we share it?" she suggests.

I'm not really hungry, and I want her to eat as much as possible, but if it'll put her at ease and coax her to eat, then I'll do it. I don't think I could ever deny her anything. If she asked me to eat mud, I'm sure I'd shovel the shit into my mouth.

I sit across from her at the table, my heart hammering in my chest as I realize this is something a normal couple would do. They would share breakfast together. This is almost like a date, yet I'm sure she doesn't see it that way.

I pick up a slice of cantaloupe and place it in my mouth, hoping to lead by example.

Riley falls right into line and picks up a strawberry, unsurprisingly. It's her favorite fruit.

My mouth goes dry as I watch her take a bite of it, her little lips curving around the fat end of the fruit. Sweet juice glistens at the corner of her lips and dribbles down to her chin. She holds her hand up to catch it and wipe it away.

I'm suddenly hard as steel in my pants and grateful for the table that's hiding my reaction to something as simple as eating. How is watching her eat a simple berry the most pornographic experience of my life?

I clear my throat and begin to make small talk to keep myself from throwing her across this table and eating *her*. I want to eat her whole.

"So are you here for Spring Break?" I ask her.

She bites into a piece of honeydew melon this time,

and I nearly groan out loud when more juice dribbles down her chin.

She nods her head. "Kinda. Well, I mean, I am. I came down here with a group of girlfriends, but I'm not really the wild, party girl type if you know what I mean. I'd much rather just sit quietly on the beach."

She blushes at her last admission like maybe she's embarrassed by that fact or something. I'm quick to put her at ease.

"Nothing wrong with that," I tell her. "I respect a girl who's not into all that heavy party scene."

I'm so glad my Riley isn't the partying type. I'll never forget the huge rush of relief that washed over me when I saw she wasn't one of the partakers of the wet T-shirt contest yesterday. Not that I thought she would be, but I had a moment of panic when I lost sight of her. I was terrified that maybe one of her friends had pushed her into going up there.

I honestly don't know what I would have done if I'd been faced with something like that. I'm sure I would have completely blown everything by stalking up there like a madman and grabbing her to stop her from revealing that body that should be for my eyes only to the entire world.

"Where do you go to school?" I continue to make small talk with her. Of course, I already know the answers to most of these questions that I'm asking her, but I ask them for her sake, to put her at ease.

Plus, there's something so captivatingly beautiful about the way her eyes light up with passion as I get the knowledge first-hand from her. When she talks about what she plans on doing with her degree, she becomes even more animated.

She wants to be a social worker and help those who've been affected by domestic violence. Although she doesn't come right out and tell me the details of what inspired her career choice, I suspect I already know. I did my homework on her, and the pieces are starting to click into place now.

Her mother's death is listed as a homicide and her father's as a suicide. I'm starting to see that maybe her father was abusive to her mother. He probably ended up killing her and then offed himself—as the piece of shit should have for hurting a woman. A man like that is too much of a coward to go to prison and face his punishment like a man. My cell block alone would have beat the shit out of him once we found out what he was in for. Hell, I'd have been the leader of the pack. There's nothing I detest more than a man who uses his strength against women. The world's better off without them, if you ask me.

As we continue to talk and eat the plate—me only taking a few tiny bites here and there just to encourage

Riley to keep eating—I notice that Riley seems to be relaxing and feeling better. Good. The drug is wearing off.

"What are you here for?" she asks me with a little curious tilt to her head.

"Oh, I'm just on a little vacation myself," I tell her. It's not exactly a lie. I suppose this is a vacation, although my main objective is to follow her on hers and make sure she's safe.

And it's a damn good thing I did too.

She asks me about myself, and I'm as honest as possible without disclosing too much. "I work on barges. It's long nights away from home and physically demanding, but it's honest work, and the pay is good."

Her eyes are wide as she regards me. "Wow, that's so cool. So you get to travel a lot?"

I shrug and she sighs. "This is the first big trip I've ever taken," she admits to me. "Before this, I've never really been beyond my hometown."

That's something we're going to rectify, I mentally tell myself. If my girl wants to travel, I'll take her to see every city in the world.

My stomach drops when she finally pushes the plate away and says, "Thanks, I'm feeling a lot better. I should probably be getting back now."

My mind races as I try to come up with a feasible way to keep her with me. "What are your plans for today?" I finally blurt out, my voice coming out much gruffer than I intend.

She blinks and then looks at me shyly. "Well, I'm probably just gonna hang around the beach. I love staring at the ocean. The water is beautiful."

I glance down at the table and notice the hotel guest book is open. There's an ad for Ponce Inlet Park. An idea pops in my head.

"What do you say we go over to the inlet? I hear the water is crystal clear there and that sometimes you can see the manatees floating up near the shore."

She looks down at where my head is motioning, taking in the ad for the inlet. It's complete with a little lighthouse and everything, though I don't give two shits about seeing the park. I just want to spend time with her.

She considers for so long a moment, I'm afraid she's going to say no, but then she finally smiles and says, "I need to grab a shower and change first."

My heart leaps within me knowing that I'm going to have more time with my precious girl. My chest is also swelling with pride at the knowledge that she's trusting me enough to go off with me like this. Not that the inlet is far, and it's a very public place. But still, I'm sure she thought she was in a public place last night too.

Surely, she knows, though. Surely, she can sense

that if I wanted to harm her, I had plenty of opportunity to do it last night, and I didn't.

I grab my car keys and hold the door open for her, feeling lighter than I've felt in ages. "Let's hop in my rental car, and I'll take you to where you're staying, little bird."

She blushes at my nickname for her. I can't help but marvel at how pretty her tanned skin looks with that pinkish glow.

I decide I'm going to keep that nickname for her.

Little bird.

My little bird.

five

. . .

Riley

The inlet is gorgeous. There's a lighthouse that's breathtaking, and there are lots of pretty boats docked in the marina.

We walk along the bridges built up over the dunes and explore all that the area has to offer. There are a couple of restaurants and tiki bars, and there are plenty of tropical-themed houses lining the streets on the way to the inlet. They're beautiful attractions in and of themselves with their stuccoed walls and pretty pastel colors.

Palm trees and hibiscus line the roads, and we even

see a raccoon or two running through the sand and into the bushes.

Parker walks me past all of that, though, and leads me over to a secluded part of the water. Yes, there are still people all around the inlet, but it's nowhere near the craziness that abounds on the main strip where Spring Break is happening at Daytona Beach.

I marvel at all the pretty shells on the shore here. The ones up at Daytona are mostly picked over by the time I go out, but there are plenty of pretty shells lying all over the shore here. There are shark teeth, scallops, and tulip shells galore, and they're not just broken pieces. They're actually intact shells.

I pick several of them up to take home with me.

I keep glancing over at Parker's big form, studying his powerful build and how his dark hair seems to shine blue in the sun.

I can't believe I'm spending time with another man —a veritable stranger—after last night.

Many people would say I'm a fool for coming out with another vacationer after what almost happened to me last night.

But somehow, I just know deep down inside that Parker would never hurt me. Besides, he had plenty of chance to do so when I was passed out in his hotel room last night if that was his intention. Yet, he didn't.

He's surprisingly easy to talk to, and I find myself

admitting things to him I've never admitted to anyone before. Like how my mom really died.

He listens to every word I say with rapt attention, his eyes never leaving me.

In one way, it's kind of unnerving, yet in another, it's so nice to be the sole focus of a man like him.

He's so big and tall and powerful, and when he takes his shirt off, I see more than one female glancing over at us, some even going so far as to give him looks of open invitation.

It bothers me, even though it shouldn't. I have no claim on him. It's not like he's my boyfriend or anything. But hell, they don't know that. What if he *was* my boyfriend? My cheeks heat at the thought.

If he was, though, and here they are leering at him right in front of me...

These bitches have no class.

To his credit, Parker's eyes never leave me. He pays none of them any mind. He just keeps looking at me in that overly intense way of his, and I'd be lying if I said having his sole attention on me doesn't fill me with a sense of smug pleasure.

I feel hot and tingly all over, and I blush every time I meet his gaze. When we're walking, sometimes he places his palm just lightly on the small of my back. I can't help noticing how big his hand is. It practically spans my whole back.

He's so much taller than me that I barely come up to his chest. He's so big where I'm so small. And I love the way he calls me "little bird." There's a note to his voice when he says it that I can't really identify. All I know is that it sends little pulses of pleasure all throughout my body. We're walking along the shore, the warm water lapping at our feet when Parker suddenly bends over and reaches down into the water.

He comes up holding a sand dollar.

I gasp. I've been wanting to find one of those ever since I got down here, and I was starting to think that I wouldn't. They're so rare, it seems, especially one that's completely intact like this one.

"For your collection," he says as he offers the sand dollar to me.

Now I'm grinning like an idiot, but I can't stop the huge smile that breaks across my face.

Just when I think this day can't get any more perfect, I see something big and dark floating through the water just a few feet from us.

I grab on to Parker's arm in my excitement. "Is that one of them?" I point to the creature moving oh so slowly through the water.

"It certainly looks like a manatee," he says after glancing over at it.

A few other people have gathered around to watch the majestic creature as it swims leisurely by us. No one's running or anything, of course, because manatees are known for their gentle nature. They're not aggressive like sharks.

"It's so beautiful," I breathe as we stand there and watch it pass by so close to us.

"Beautiful," Parker echoes my sentiment, but when I look up at him, he's not looking at the manatee.

He's looking at me.

I suddenly realize that I'm still clinging to his arm, my body pressed up against the side of his. My face flashes, and I start to step away from him, but his arm bands around me, holding me next to him.

He's staring down at me with that intense look on his face, his eyes like gray coals.

"Parker?" I breathe his name, not knowing what I'm going to say, but my God, his head is moving down toward me. His lips are getting closer and closer to mine. I begin to tremble. Is he about to kiss me?

"Riley." He breathes my name whenever he's just a hair's breadth away from my lips.

I feel his minty breath fanning over my lips, and I lick them instinctively.

He makes some sort of strangled sound that's a half growl, half groan, and then before I can fully register what's happening, his lips come down on mine.

———

Parker

Sweet. Like pure fucking sugar.

I knew my little bird would taste delicious, but I wasn't prepared for just how sweet she is. I angle her head up to me as I slip my tongue inside her mouth and tangle it with hers.

She kisses me back hesitantly, innocently, and damn if that doesn't turn me on more than the most practiced kiss.

It makes me dare to hope that she's never been touched by anyone else. Of course, I know she hasn't dated since I've been watching her—not before I went to prison, nor since I've gotten out. But I'm not sure about the time when I was locked up or before that day she first graced me with her smile.

I kiss her deeper, jealousy spurring me to show her that she's *mine*.

She melts against me, and I inwardly curse myself that we're here on this very public beach.

I need her alone. *Now.*

I somehow get myself under control enough to pull back from her.

Her lips are pink and swollen from our kiss. I stroke my thumbs gently over her cheeks as her eyelashes flutter open. Her pretty blue eyes slam right into me, squeezing my chest with their shining luminescence.

They're deeper than the ocean, and I want to explore their depths. I'd gladly drown in them if it meant I could get closer to the core of who she is.

She blushes when she comes back to her senses and realizes I just kissed her here in front of all these people. Her eyes dart around, but no one is staring at us. They're tastefully looking away and giving us a front of privacy. She looks back up at me and bites her lip, fighting back a smile before she looks down again.

I have to stop thinking about how sweet her lips taste or I'm going to embarrass myself with a raging hard-on here on this beach.

I clear my throat and ask her, "Are you hungry, little bird?"

She looks back up at me. The wind catches tendrils of her hair and sends it spiraling around her face. She pushes it back with one hand and then smiles up at me. "Yeah."

I walk her over to the restaurant, and we're seated at one of the private outdoor tables. There's a backed bench on each side of the table and a tiki-style canopy over our heads to shade us from the sun.

I watch her sigh as she slides onto the bench and looks out over our fantastic view of the water. I follow her line of sight. This view is beautiful, but it's nothing like the view I get staring at her.

"It really is paradise," she murmurs.

"Yes," I agree, still looking at her. This place might be her paradise, but she's mine.

When the waiter comes to order our drinks, I tense at the way he looks at Riley. His smile is a little too friendly for my taste. It falters when he catches my death glare.

My scowl only deepens when he calls me "sir." I realize that's standard address for any male customer, but my irrationally jealous brain is taking it as an insult—like the little prick is pointing out that I'm older than both him and Riley and that he's closer to her age than I am.

I notice that Riley doesn't order an alcoholic drink. I follow suit and order a lemonade like she did. I'm pleased she's being wary of drinking now. It shows that she's careful and more aware after last night.

My jaw clenches at the thought of the asshole. I still have to deal with him.

"Are you okay?" Riley's voice breaks into my dark thoughts. She's looking at me with concern, and I force myself to relax.

"Of course." I reach across the table to take her tiny hand in mine. I love the way my hand completely dwarfs hers. "Why wouldn't I be? I'm sitting in paradise with the most beautiful girl in the world."

It's a cheesy line, but I don't mean it as a line. I'm just speaking the truth and telling her how I feel.

Her cheeks turn that delightful shade of pink that I love, and she gives me a soft smile before saying, "Thank you for bringing me out here. Today has been amazing."

"I'm the one who should be thanking you," I tell her honestly. "It's not always so fun exploring places on my own. I appreciate the company."

"We could see more places together if you want," she suggests. My mouth goes dry, and my heart's beating loudly in my ears. Riley wants more contact with me. It's everything I've been yearning for, and it's like it's too good to be true.

Her face turns red when I'm silent, and she pulls her hand away to cover her cheeks in embarrassment. "I mean, only if you want to. All I'm saying is I'm here for a few more days, and today is the best day I've had so far, and you said it's not so fun exploring on your own. I just thought"—she bites her lip—"that we could, you know, explore together."

My chest is tight as I take in how absolutely adorable she looks when she's flustered.

"As friends," she adds quickly, like maybe I think she's asking me on a date and that's what's holding me back.

Holding her eyes with my own, I reach across the table and take both of her hands in mine, suddenly done holding back. Time to lay all my cards on the table. "I'll spend every day with you if you want, Riley, but I want to be more than just friends."

Her eyes widen, and that pretty blush creeps over her face and neck again.

The waiter returns then with our drinks and to take our orders.

I don't even know what I order. It's inconsequential. I just tell him to bring me whatever she's having because I can't tear my gaze away from her long enough to even look down at my menu.

She's my pretty little bird, and she's actually flying straight toward me.

six

. . .

Riley

Parker and I spend the next few days exploring all that Volusia County has to offer. We go to De Leon Springs State Park. We go to Blue Springs State Park. We mosey through the Museum of Arts and Sciences.

We find new beach spots, some in Port Orange and some in North Daytona, but our favorite is at New Smyrna Beach.

New Smyrna has the most secluded patches of beach land. We were able to find spots where we couldn't see anyone for miles.

There's something so surreal about sitting on the

beach alone with Parker. Although he hasn't pressed for more than kisses, my body is always buzzing when I'm wrapped up in his arms. We like to sit with my back to his front and his arms wrapped around me as we look out at the waves.

Sometimes we sit in companionable silence, each lost in our own thoughts as we watch the tide roll in.

I don't know what's going to happen when Spring Break is over and we both go our separate ways.

We haven't talked about it. I don't like pondering it, so I don't. I just live in the moment and enjoy each second with my dark angel—because that's what I've come to think of him as.

Parker saved me that night. And while he might come across as dark and brooding and mysterious to other people, I've gotten to know him.

He's really gentle and kind, and I know he would never do anything to hurt me.

In fact, he's been a perfect gentleman. I can feel his hardness between us when he kisses me, but he never pressures me for more—even though I think I want more with him.

I've never been with anyone in that way before, but imagining Parker being the one to make me a woman sends little tingles of desire rushing throughout me.

"Look, Riley." Parker's arms band closer about me

as he lifts his arm and points straight ahead out to the water.

I gasp as I see gray fins bobbing up out of the water.

"Are those sharks?" I ask him in amazement.

"Keep watching," he says. I feel him plant a kiss on the side of my temple, and then I see a bunch of gray fins grouped up together, bobbing up and out of the water over and over again.

"They're dolphins," he whispers into my ear, his voice tickling my skin and sending delicious shivers up and down my spine.

"Wow," I breathe, wishing I could get a closer look at them. "So beautiful," I marvel.

"Yes," Parker agrees, although when I tilt my head back to look at him, once again, he's not looking at what I'm looking at. He's looking at *me*.

A thrill runs through me at the heated look in his eyes. A lock of his dark hair falls down over his forehead as he lowers his head to capture my lips.

He sucks on my bottom lip before his tongue begins probing, seeking entry to my mouth.

I open to him readily, kissing him back.

I love kissing him. I could do this forever. I bask in the connection that lights up between us whenever our tongues are twining together like this. It's like there's a tether connecting my soul to his. I've never felt closer to anyone in my entire life as I do this man.

Emboldened by the intimacy wrapping around us, I break free of his kiss and turn to straddle his lap before smashing my lips back down on his, kissing him more aggressively than I've ever kissed him.

He growls into my mouth in response before fisting his hand in my hair and taking charge. His kiss becomes demanding and desperate. It's consuming me, and I feel his hardness pulsing right at the apex of my thighs.

I don't know what comes over me, but I began to rock my hips against him, sliding my bikini-clad mound up and down his length. Pleasure snaps from that point between my legs and shoots straight up to my core.

I whimper at the sensation as Parker deepens our kiss and thrusts his hips up against me before his hands suddenly light on my own hips, stilling me.

"Riley, baby," he rasps against my lips, "if you keep that up, God help me, I'm not going to be able to stop, honey."

I cant my hips against him by way of answer. I don't want him to stop.

He makes a feral sound when he realizes what I'm wordlessly saying. His arms tighten around me posses- sively. It's like all the control he's been showing all week suddenly snaps. His hands and lips are all over me, trailing down over my neck and the tops of my shoulders, along the inside of my arms.

He cups my breasts through my bikini top. "Been dying to taste these little cherries," he rasps against my collarbone as he trails kisses down to the triangles of my bikini top. He moves the tiny scraps of fabric aside to expose my hard nipples. "You just don't know how long," he adds before taking one in his mouth.

I gasp and arch up into him, fire shooting straight to that aching place between my legs. His tongue swirls around one and then the other as he takes turns sucking each of them into his mouth.

I've never felt anything like this, and I can't think. All I can do is throw my head back and feel the deliciousness of his mouth feeding from me.

All the while his hands are still moving over my skin, traveling down my stomach and to that place between my legs. His fingers slip under the band of my bikini bottoms, and he hisses in a breath when he finds my wetness.

My cheeks color in embarrassment, but he makes it clear that he loves just how wet I am by growling, "Look at how wet this pussy is for me, baby. I'm going to eat you whole, Riley. Gonna eat you up, honey."

I feel myself clench, gripping at air, at his words.

He's licking and sucking at the side of my neck now,

sending a new ripple of sensations all throughout me while his hand delves in between my folds and finds this little place that makes me arch into him and moan. Every swipe of his finger over the slippery bud sends snaps of pleasure rippling straight to my stomach, and my empty hole starts to ache, longing to be filled. Filled with him.

"Have you ever come before, baby?" he asks me, lust hooding his eyes.

I shake my head. "No." I blush at my admission, realizing how babyish I probably sound to have never experienced an orgasm at my age.

However, that knowledge seems to please him because his eyes dilate and his nostrils flare before he smashes his lips back onto mine again.

"Your first orgasm is going to be on my cock," he growls into my mouth. "Do you hear me, little bird?"

"Yes," I answer him back breathlessly, wanting that more than anything now.

"Gonna make you mine in every way," he says, his voice low and husky as he unties the strings holding up my bikini bottoms and then frees himself from his swimming trunks.

My eyes widen when I take in the sheer size of him. His girth is swollen, angry, and pulsing, and I see a bit of moisture on the tip.

He doesn't give me long to admire him before he's lifting me up and lining himself up at my entrance.

"Can't wait," he grits out. I feel his hand trembling where he holds my hips steady. "Gonna make you mine."

Something about the way he says he wants to make me his sends more wetness pooling between my thighs.

He pops the tip inside me, and I gasp at the sudden fullness, the stretching of having him inside me, and I know he's not even all the way there. It's just the tip.

I start to panic and tense up.

"Riley, look at me," he demands.

My eyes snap to his, and I bite my lip at the fire I see blazing in his gray orbs. He's panting like he's just run a marathon. Every sinew in his arm and chest is taut. Blue glistens in his hair as the sun hits it.

He's so beautiful, my dark angel, and I want to be his in every way.

"You're so beautiful, baby," he praises me as he holds my eyes captive.

Then, he's plunging up into me and pulling me down onto him simultaneously.

It happens so quickly. Pain sears through me. Something within me breaks and gives way.

"Fuck!" we both cry out as he seats himself fully inside me.

I'm clinging to him and try to control my breathing, focusing on taking in deep breaths. God, it feels like he ripped me in two, but the worst of it is over, I know.

He strokes his hands down my back and mumbles sweet nothings to me about how good I did and how perfect I am, and I relax under the soothing timbre of his voice.

The pain finally starts to fade away just as he groans and begins to make probing little thrusts inside me.

The sensation of his huge girth sliding against my walls creates this delicious friction. The head of his cock is hitting this place deep inside me that sends a tickling sensation right below my belly button. It builds a pressure deep within me.

I start pushing back down onto him, seeking more of that wonderful sensation.

"Damn, Riley," he rasps out against my ear as he begins pounding up into me harder. The sounds he's making are causing a thrill to run through me, his guttural grunts and groans pulling at something deep inside me.

Sweat breaks out on both our skin, and we're both panting as we rock together seeking the same release.

"Tell me you're mine," he suddenly demands as he grabs the back of my neck and forces me to look at him.

There's a feral look in his eyes that sends a primitive rush of excitement through me. There's something thrilling about knowing I've got him all worked up like this.

"I'm yours," I agree, promising myself to him.

"Fuck, Riley, baby," he pants out as he strokes in and out of me desperately. "You just don't know. I'm never going to be able to let you go now."

My heart melts at his admission.

"Then don't," I urge him, not wanting him to let me go either.

"Gonna keep you forever." His voice is barely more than a growl. "Claim you as mine. When I bust this big nut in you, there's never going to be anyone else for you. You hear me, little bird?"

I don't get to answer him because his possessive words send me spiraling over the edge. Something bursts deep inside me, and then I'm crashing down onto him like the waves on the shore.

"Oh fuck, look at how beautiful you are when you come all over my cock, honey." He makes a strangled sound before he lets out a roar and holds himself deep inside me.

I feel his release shoot up into me in thick spurts. The sensation pushes me into another wave of ripples.

He's pulsing inside me while I'm spasming around him. We're shaking in each other's arms.

He grabs my hair and takes my lips again, kissing me possessively.

"Riley, Riley, Riley." He's chanting my name like a little prayer. "Little bird, my sweet little bird. Mine, mine, mine."

I cling to him, basking in the feeling of him holding me safe in his arms.

His, his, his, my own mind is chanting. *Always and forever.*

seven

. . .

Parker

I meant what I told Riley. They weren't just words spoken in the heat of passion. I'm never going to be able to let her go now. Not now that she's mine, finally all mine.

It humbles me to think of her having her first orgasm on *my* cock. I start getting hard just remembering how beautiful she looked when she came with me buried deep inside her.

I'm not spending another night away from her. She's coming back to my hotel with me.

First, I need to feed my little bird, though.

We share a nice, intimate dinner at a little restaurant right on the beach where we watch the sun set over the ocean. Well, the sun doesn't actually set over the Atlantic. It sets over the Pacific. But we watch the pink and amber colors streaking across the sky as the sun goes down off in the distance.

I never took myself for one of those beach-loving guys. I've never been big on vacations. And part of it is because of what I told Riley earlier. It's just not fun to travel and explore places on your own.

But now I'll always have a soft spot for the beach. This is the place where I finally got to insert myself into Riley's life and make her mine in every way. The first time I became one with my girl, with nothing but the blue sky above us, the sand underneath us, and the roaring of the waves crashing over us in tempo with our passion.

It's an experience I'll hold with me until my dying day—and even beyond.

I could stay here forever in this paradise with her. And it's not the place that makes it paradise. It's *her*. It's everything about her.

She could drag me to the depths of hell, and it would be paradise so long as I was with her.

My sweet little bird, my angel.

She smiles at me now as I rub my thumb in circles

on her palm. I can't stop touching her. It's like now that she's given herself to me, I'm a glutton. I can't get enough.

I can't wait to get her back to my hotel room and make love to her all night long and in every position imaginable. I'm going to eat her for an hour straight until she comes all over my face. I'm going to make love to her until she can't take it anymore and breaks all over me.

And then I'm going to fuck her until she begs me to stop. She'll be so full of me that she'll never be able to think of another man.

Mine. I know I just claimed her, and I know I'm the only man she's ever been with, but I still have this primal need to keep reasserting my claim on her—to make sure she's mine and only mine.

I've wanted this for so long. I've wanted *her* for so long. It's like I'm afraid that something's going to come along and snatch this all away from me.

Over my dead body.

When we finish eating, Riley excuses herself to go to the restroom.

I throw some bills on the table to cover the tab and then mosey over to lean my elbow against the railing of the outdoor patio deck as I watch my girl heading inside.

I frown when a man comes barreling out of the restaurant just as she opens the door.

He bumps into her, but I see her utter an apology like she's the one who ran into him. My jaw clenches. I hate her apologizing for things that aren't her fault. My Riley is too sweet for her own good.

The asshole scowls down at her before sauntering over to where I'm standing. He shakes his head mumbling, "Clumsy bitch."

I tense and glare at him, silently daring him to say another word against my precious little bird. He glances over and sees me eyeing him. He either has a death wish or is just thick as shit and can't sense danger when it's staring him right in the face because he opens his insolent mouth and adds another insult to his crime. "Stupid bitches, all they're good for is choking on some cock. Don't you agree?" He raises his eyebrow at me like we're frat buddies and he's waiting for me to agree and fist-bump him.

My vision goes red at his disrespectful words. They're barely out of his mouth before I snap, grabbing him by the collar and baring my teeth at him in an inhuman growl.

Nobody talks about my Riley that way.

———

Riley

As amazing as this evening has been, I'm kind of sad because I don't want it to end.

I wonder if Parker is going to ask me back to his place. I'm not ready to say goodbye to him for the night. I don't really want to go back to my hotel room with the girls.

Not that the girls aren't great. They know I've been seeing someone, and there's been plenty of teasing about it, and I'm sure that that will only amplify if I don't come home tonight, but I don't care. I just want to be with Parker.

I head back out toward the beachside patio ready to just tell him how I feel when I stop dead in my tracks at the sight before me.

People are staring in shock at the man who's pummeling another man to death. Blood is flying everywhere, and the man throwing the hits is letting out inhuman roars of rage.

He's like an unhinged beast.

An icy shiver goes down my spine when I read realize the unhinged beast is Parker.

I shrink back as the wrath in his eyes and the curl to his lips sends me spiraling back into the past.

I'm suddenly a young girl again, hunkered down in the

corner with my hands slapped over my ears to try to drown out the sobbing from my mother and the screaming of my father as he wails down on her.

I don't even know what he's mad at her about. I never understand what he's mad at her about. Just sometimes he comes home and just goes crazy and starts hitting her.

I begin to tremble as that feeling of helplessness washes over me once again.

"Stop!" I scream as I close my eyes and clap my hands over my ears, trying to drown out the sound.

When I open my eyes, it's not my mother and father I see, though. It's Parker and everyone else in the restaurant staring at me.

I look at the man I just gave myself to, the man I'm pretty sure I've fallen in love with.

His knuckles are covered in blood, and he's still holding the other man up by the scruff of his shirt, his chest heaving. His gray eyes are stormier than the storm clouds that have suddenly rolled in off the ocean.

I can't reconcile the image of the violent man in front of me with the gentle man I've come to know over the past week.

I let out a sob as I turn and run from the restaurant, fighting to pull my phone out of my little beach bag that's slung over my shoulder so I can call a cab to take me far away from here and all this madness.

"Riley! Wait!" I hear Parker's voice calling for me, but that only spurs me on harder.

Before I can even dial the number for a taxi, I see one idling on the road up ahead. I sprint to it and then launch myself into the backseat, barking out the name of my hotel before urging him to go.

Apparently, he can see that I'm in a hurry because he jumps into action and speeds off from the curb.

I glance through the back window of the taxi and see Parker running behind us, his mouth moving as he tries to chase us down.

Tears stream down my cheeks, and I force myself to turn back around and away from the man I was so close to giving my everything too, a violent man who's not at all who I thought he was. My mind replays the images of Parker beating the shit out of that guy in the restaurant. Every time I think of it, I can't stop thinking about my mother and father and their volatile relationship.

My mother married a violent man, and look at what happened to her. He murdered her.

My heart twists within me when I think of Parker. It's telling me to stop, that there's no way he would ever hurt me.

But my eyes just showed me how violent he can get.

I remember very well how much my mother loved

my father—so much so that despite how he hurt her, she always gave him one more chance when he apologized.

Until one day that one more chance was one too many.

I remember her telling me he wasn't like that in the beginning, that he'd been the perfect guy.

Until he wasn't.

I thought Parker was perfect and kind and gentle until I saw him unleash his violence just now. My heart and mind are torn, pulling me in two different directions.

I don't really know what I should do, but I know one thing.

I refuse to be my mother.

That's why I go with my mind. The heart is blind and doesn't sense danger as well as the mind does. I'm not going to make my mother's mistake and listen to my heart over my mind.

As much as this is killing me, I'm going to put Parker behind me and move on with my life. Besides, isn't this what was always going to happen? When Spring Break is over, we were always going to go our separate ways, back to our own lives.

It never would have worked out between us anyway.

He was just a Spring Break fling—nothing else.

That's what I try to tell myself to stave the aching in my heart.

But if that's true, why is my chest so tight, and why do these tears keep falling?

eight

. . .

Parker

"Fuck!" I scream as I pound my fist into the wall.

I've tried calling Riley's phone over and over again, but it keeps going straight to voicemail. She's purposefully ignoring me.

When I went to her hotel, her friends were like guard dogs and wouldn't let me in the room, telling me that she didn't want to see me and even going so far as to threaten to call the police if I didn't leave.

I'm pacing back and forth in my own hotel room while fisting my hands in my hair.

I'm frantic. My chest is squeezing, and I feel like I can't breathe.

I'm dying here without her.

I had her. She was mine. She gave herself to me.

And then I had to go and lose control.

It was my violence that did it.

I already know that's why she's frightened of me all of a sudden. And no wonder after what her father did to her mother.

But damn it, doesn't she know I would never hurt her? The only time I'm ever violent is when it's to protect her, and that's what I was doing back there, protecting her.

It's only a matter of time before she finds out the rest. I never told her about how I went to prison. Her friends are probably running a background check on me now, convinced that I'm some serial killer or psycho.

It was always going to come out, and I wasn't purposefully hiding it from her. Well, I was, but I wasn't going to forever. I was going to tell her eventually. Ideally, after we'd known each other a little bit longer.

She's not going to see it that way, though. She's just going to see me as the felon who duped her into giving him her virginity. She's going to think that I was just using her when in reality all I've ever really wanted in my entire life is her. Everything I've ever done since that first day she smiled at me was for her.

I can't believe I fucked this up so badly. My arms are literally aching to hold her. Lord Tennyson was an idiot. It's not better to have loved and lost than to have never loved at all. It's torture.

He'd obviously never loved a woman like Riley. It's torture to have had her and then to not have her because now I truly know what I'm missing.

I finally force myself to stop pacing. I brace my hands on my knees and take in deep breaths to calm myself.

Riley's just shaken up because I triggered her memories. She's still mine. She gave herself to me.

And that is a promise I'm going to hold her to.

If she needs some space, that's fine. I'll go back to watching her from the shadows like I've always done, and when she's ready for me, I'll be here.

I'll wait as long as she needs to prove myself to her. Because that's true love. I'll never give up on her. I'll give her space, but I'll be there to protect her too—like I've always done.

Riley is mine.

———

Riley

Spring Break vacation was cut short by my little fiasco with Parker. I feel bad because the girls gave up the last few days of their vacation to come home early because of me. But that just goes to show how we might not be super close, but they're good friends when it counts. They were worried about a violent man being after me, especially when they pulled his record and saw that he's been to prison.

The betrayal that knifed through me at finding that out left a cut so deep I don't know if it will ever heal.

I thought I knew Parker. I thought we had this amazing connection. Come to find out, he's been keeping all these secrets from me.

He went to jail for violently assaulting a couple of guys and nearly beating them to death.

When I saw his arrest record staring back at me, it was hard to imagine him being so violent, but I saw it with my own eyes.

But then I remember how tenderly he kissed me and how gentle his hands were on my skin. He held me like I was made of glass, like I was something delicate and precious.

But what if the way he held me so possessively was just the beginning of an obsessive, toxic relationship like the one my parents had?

Something deep inside me is telling me that me and

Parker's relationship is nothing like the one my parents had, but that fear is still there. I can't shake it.

To make matters worse, ever since I've gotten back to college, those little prickles at the back of my neck have returned. That sensation of being watched went away when I was with Parker. Maybe that's just because I was so wrapped up in him I couldn't see anything else.

And as much as I know it might not be healthy, as much as I hate to admit it, I miss the man I got to know —whether he was real or not.

Every day I find myself remembering all the things we did on the beach together and how great it felt just to sit quietly in each other's presence. It's like we've known each other our whole lives.

But I didn't really know him, did I?

My nights are filled with dreams of our bodies moving together on the beach. I can't forget that soul-deep connection I felt when we were joined as one person, and I wake up wet and frustrated and aching.

Maybe I'm putting too much stock in it. Maybe it was just sex.

But I remember the intensity in his eyes when he insisted on seeing my face while he was inside me. How could he fake such feeling?

But no, maybe he didn't fake it, but that still doesn't mean he's not violent and that those violent tendencies won't bleed over into our relationship if I allow us to have one.

I shake my head as tears prick my eyes again. It was too good to be true. I should have known better.

My restless nights and my frazzled emotions are taking a toll on me. I'm a wreck during the day. I can hardly bring myself to eat, and there are bags under my eyes. I'm moping around, more depressed than I've ever been in my entire life.

My roommate calls me out on it one day, insisting that I go out with her and the girls for a night out on the town. She swears it will do me good to get out and have a night of drinking and just forget all of this.

While I'm totally not feeling up to it, I don't have the energy to fight her. Besides, who knows? Maybe it really will help me. I know nothing else is working. No matter how much I try to forget about him, I just can't.

It's like he's stained into my memory, and no amount of scrubbing will remove him.

nine

. . .

Parker

I snarl when I see one of the men from the club step up to her.

No way. Not happening.

Whether she still acknowledges it or not, she's mine, and I'll be damned if I stand here and let another man touch her. My lips press into a thin line, and rage pulses throughout my veins when I see him hand her a cup. My fury only compounds whenever she accepts it and takes a tiny sip.

He places his hand on her hip and begins to pull her closer, and that's when I really lose it. I push through the throng of dancers and doggedly make my way over to her.

I grab the cup from her hand and slam it down on the bar. "Did you not learn your lesson last time?" I snap at her as I grab the man's arm and fling it off her.

"Hey, dude, what the—?" he begins, but I bare my teeth at him ferally, and he holds his hands up, backing off. "Look, no harm, no foul. I didn't realize she was taken, I swear."

Pussy. I glance at him in disgust, but I don't dignify him with a response.

I turn my full attention back on my girl. And that's right. Riley is still *my* girl. She's *mine.* Always has been, always will be.

If she's not going to be with me, she's not going to be with anyone. We'll both be fucking miserable. Is it a dick move? Yes, but the alternative is me murdering any man she hooks up with, so we'll both just have to sacrifice for the greater good.

She's staring up at me with wide eyes, and her face goes pale like she's seen a ghost.

Shit. I run a hand over my face wearily. I probably shouldn't have led out my next time seeing her face to face by snapping at her.

"Are you following me?" she finally asks when she gets her wits back about her enough to do so.

"We need to talk," I tell her instead of answering

her. I take her hand and begin pulling her to one of the back rooms of the club.

She resists, pulling against my hand. "I'm not going anywhere with you," she hisses at me.

I ignore her and continue to pull her along with me, desperate to speak to her, desperate to make her understand I would never hurt her.

I'm going crazy without her, and seeing another man's hands on her just sealed the deal.

I thought I could stay away from her and just watch from the shadows, but I can't. I can't do that anymore. I need her.

I need her in my life to breathe, to keep me sane. She's got to see that.

I finally yank us into an empty room. Her chest is heaving, and her little breasts are pushed up on display in the skin-tight red dress she's wearing. It's much too short for my liking, showing off her long legs. Riley might be a petite little thing, but her legs seem to go on forever.

"I don't like it," I growl at her as I take a step toward her.

She doesn't ask what I don't like, but I tell her anyway, "That dress shows off too much of what's mine."

I take another step toward her and see her tremble.

My chest tightens. Is my little bird really that afraid of me? Does she think I'm a monster?

She licks her lips, and her voice comes out shaky when she warns, "I'll scream."

Another step toward her, and she opens her mouth to let out a shrill shriek.

My eyebrows shoot up to my hairline. Damn, she wasn't kidding. I react without thinking, slamming my mouth down onto hers and capturing her cry in my mouth, sucking it down into my lungs.

Her cry turns into a sob as I wrap her in my arms and pull her flush against me, her entire frame trembling.

Sobs begin to wrack her entire body, and I tighten my arms around her, holding her close as she breaks down. I pull back just enough to stroke her hair and try to soothe her.

"That's it, little bird. Let it all out. Give it all to me. Let me take all the pain away." She sobs harder, burying her head in my chest, and I just hold her, stroking her soothingly, offering her what little comfort I can, hating that I'm the cause of her pain.

"What do you want me to do, baby?" I ask her desperately. "Whatever you need, I'll do it. I'll cut off my arm if it'll just make you feel better." I'm not being dramatic. I really will if she wants me to. I'll do anything she wants.

Her cheeks are tear-stained when she finally pulls back and looks up at me with watery eyes. "I can't do this, Parker. I just can't. I can't be my mother."

She shakes her head as if just remembering that I'm not supposed to be here. "How are you even here? How did you find me?"

I take in a deep breath before I take her face in my palms and stare right into her beautiful blue eyes as I bare my entire truth to her. "I've been watching you for years, Riley. I know you don't remember me, but you bumped into me one day when I was coming home from the docks. I'd had a shitty trip, and you smiled at me. That beautiful fucking smile of yours." I shake my head and let out an exhale at the memory. Just the thought of that first smile from this beautiful girl still takes my breath away. "It lit something inside of me. You were so goddamned beautiful, a light shining in my darkness. And I couldn't let that light get away, so I followed you. You were waitressing at that little dive bar down by the docks. You remember that?"

Her eyes are wide as she nods at me dazedly like she can't believe I knew her from way back then.

I continue, needing to confess everything now that I've started, "It's true. I've been to prison, little bird, but it's not because I'm just some violent person who has anger management issues. Some guys were getting handsy with you in the bar, and when the manager threw them out, I overheard them plotting about what they planned to do to you when you got off work."

My throat works, and my hands want to clench into fists at just the memory of it, so I drop them from her face. The anger I feel welling up in me even now at the memory is too volatile for me to touch her with it coursing through me.

I look back down into her eyes, pleading with her to understand. "I couldn't let them hurt you, honey, so I stopped them. I got caught, and I did my time for it."

She's completely silent for a moment. When she does speak, her voice is barely more than an incredulous whisper. "You went to prison for me?"

I nod. "I'd do it all again if it meant keeping you safe."

"I'm sorry," she apologizes to me, her eyes glistening with tears.

"How many times have I told you not to apologize for the actions of other people?" I gently reprimand her. "It wasn't your fault at all, little bird. You're my one weakness, Riley. I lose my temper when it comes to defending you."

"But you went to prison because of me. That's so awful." Guilt is written all over her face, and she looks down.

"Hey." I tilt her head back up to me, forcing her to meet my eyes. "The worst part of it was knowing that

I'd left you out here all alone. You don't know what kind of torture that was, worried about what was going to happen to you while I was locked up in there. I prayed every day to any deity that would listen just to keep you safe long enough for me to get out and watch over you again."

She bites her lips, looking up at me with a dawning comprehension. "You're the one who's been following me."

I nod. "You always sensed me. I saw it."

Her brow furrows. "Why didn't you just show yourself and explain?"

It's my turn to not meet her eyes. "I know I'm not good enough for you, Riley. I'm a felon, and I didn't want to scare you."

"That guy at the restaurant…" she begins slowly.

My jaw clenches as I explain, "He said something derogatory about you. I couldn't let that slide."

Her eyes search mine, tears glistening in them once again.

I take her hands in mine and bring them up to my lips, kissing her knuckles reverently. "I understand your fear, baby, because of what you saw your father do to your mother, but I swear to you, little bird, I would never hurt you. You must know that. I worship you. All I want to do is keep you safe, keep your mine."

I implore her to hear the truth in my words and see it reflected in my eyes.

Tears roll down her cheeks again as new understanding lights her eyes. I wipe them away with the pads of my thumbs.

"I've missed you," she finally admits.

And suddenly all the tightness in my chest finally dissipates as relief washes over me. I haven't completely lost her.

I pull her close to me again, savoring the feeling of having her in my arms where she belongs.

"I missed you too, honey, more than you'll ever know." She leans into me, and I take her lips in another kiss, this one showing her all the pent-up hunger I have for her.

"You don't know the torture I've been in watching you and not being able to have you," I rasp against her lips as I move my hands down along that little red dress, suddenly desperate to have her.

My fingers skim the hem of it and pull it up just enough to reveal the matching red thong she has on. I hiss in a breath when I see how it fits against her puffy little mound.

I fall to my knees before her and pull her panties to the side so I can lick her from slit to clit.

"Parker!" She gasps my name as her tiny hands fist in my hair.

"This pussy is going to be the death of me," I tell her as I continue to lick her. She's just as sweet there as she is everywhere else, and I've been dying for a taste.

I rub her little nub with my thumb, just as I thrust my tongue up inside her hole.

She cries out as she comes, spasming around my tongue and bathing my face with her sweet juices.

I'm hard as a rock and can't wait to be inside her. I pick her up and slam her back against the wall as I undo my pants and thrust into her tight heat.

"Oh God!" she cries out as she bangs her head back against the wall.

I grab the nape of her neck and pull her head back to look directly into my eyes. "No, my little bird. It's only you and me here. Just you and me."

I hold our eye contact as I pump inside her, giving her all I've got, showing her with my body how much I need and want her.

I feel the waves of her release crash over us. She's dripping down my length and convulsing all around me, her wet, silky heat milking me until I spill up into her.

I roar as I pump my load into her, each pulse sending a new wave of pleasure over me as I paint her womb with my seed.

Somewhere in the back of my mind, I register that we've never used protection, and the thought that she could get pregnant with my child sends more sticky ropes jetting up my stalk.

I slump against her when my balls are finally spent. "I love you, Riley," I confess as I drop kisses all over her face, unable to hold back the intensity of my feelings for this woman.

"I love you too, Parker," her sweet little voice says in my ear.

"Tell me you'll never run from me again, little bird," I beg her, needing to hear her say the words.

"I promise," she vows, her crystal blue eyes holding mine. They're filled with more love and understanding and forgiveness than I deserve, but selfish bastard that I am, I'll take it. I'll take it all and then some. I greedily want all of her, and in return, I'll give her all of me.

"I'm yours"—her sweet breath fans across my lips —"now and forever."

My soul soars. What more could I ever ask for?

epilogue

. . .

Three years later

Riley

I hug the woman standing before me before I give her a care packet filled with everything she needs to give her a fresh, safe start away from her abusive partner. I finished getting my degree a couple of years ago, although I had to finish it up by taking online classes since Parker and I quickly found out we were pregnant after we made our relationship official.

Of course, all of the girls I went to Spring Break

with thought I was crazy when they found out Parker and I were together—that is, until I told them the full story of what he did for me. Then they were all swooning and talking about how romantic it all was.

I eventually drifted away from them. We all went our separate ways after college. They moved off, and I did too. Parker and I fell in love with Florida where our romance officially started and decided to move to Volusia County, though we have a home tucked away in the privacy of New Smyrna Beach far away from all the annual Spring Break festivities neither of us ever really cared for.

Anyway, while I was freaking out about the pregnancy, Parker was thrilled. He assured me he had enough money put away to take care of us and the baby, and it's true. Parker is a wonderful provider.

Still, my career choice isn't about money. It's about honoring my mother's memory and helping people.

And I've done one better than what I originally planned to do. I originally planned on working as a social worker for the state, but Parker helped me start my own outreach program. I can run things my way, and I'm able to reach lots more people this way.

Although I'm a working mom, Parker picks up the slack. He doesn't work the barges anymore. He can't bear to be away from me or little Molly for that long, and although I'd have supported anything he wanted to do, I'm secretly relieved he chose not to go off to sea anymore.

I can't bear the thought of being parted from my husband for weeks on end either.

Parker watches our sweet baby girl and teaches self-defense part time as part of one of my center's programs.

My heart swells when I lock the doors and step back to take in the business that my husband and I built together. We're a great team.

And speaking of my husband…

I feel a little prickle at the base of my spine and turn to find him watching me.

I can always sense him when he's nearby. Even before I knew who he was, I was never really alone. He was always there watching me. Love and gratitude wells up within me at the thought.

I wouldn't be where I am today were it not for him. This amazing man who was willing to do jail time to protect a girl who didn't even know he existed.

"Hey, little bird." He leans down to greet me with a kiss before holding the door to our SUV open.

"Hey, yourself." I kiss him back eagerly, already feeling desire stirring in me.

"I have a surprise for you tonight," he tells me with a little twinkle in his eye as he starts the car and pulls off onto the highway.

Instead of turning right to go toward our home, he turns onto A1A, the highway that lines the beachfront.

I glance over at him questioningly, wondering what he's up to.

"How's Molly been today?" I ask him, already missing my little girl.

"She's great." He goes on to tell me about some of the antics she got into that day, his eyes lighting up with fatherly pride. The sight of his love for our daughter only endears him to me even more. "She was already tucked into bed when I left her with the babysitter," he assures me.

I try to ignore the prick of disappointment I feel at not getting to see her tonight, but two nights a week, we stay open late, so I know I'll get to see my little girl tomorrow.

"Parker, where are you taking us?" I ask him, my curiosity getting the better of me.

He just grins over at me, refusing to divulge his secrets.

I huff and feign hurt, but he just laughs.

Finally, he pulls off the road and parks in a familiar parking lot. It's completely empty right now. The streetlights are on, and stars are twinkling up in the sky when we get out of the car.

My husband takes my hand and walks me out onto the sand.

I smile as the sound of the waves crashing washes over me and the salty tang of the sea air teases my nostrils.

Parker drapes a beach towel on the sand and then sits us down, wrapping his arms around me from behind. I melt back into him, loving the feeling of his strong arms around me.

His voice is low and husky as he speaks directly into my ear. "Do you recognize this place, little bird?"

"Of course I do," I reply softly. It's the place where Parker took my virginity.

"And do you know what today is?" He places a kiss on the shell of my ear, and I tilt my head to look back at him questioningly.

"It's the anniversary of that day," he tells me softly.

My eyes widen. Yeah, I know when our wedding anniversary is, of course, but I didn't realize Parker kept up with the anniversary of the first day we made love.

A smile curves my lips as I do just like I did that day three years ago and turn in his arms to straddle him. "Let me guess," I tease him. "You want to make me yours again?"

His hold tightens on my hips as he growls, "You're already mine, but I'll never tire of claiming you again, *wife*."

My heart skips a beat at the possessive way he says

"wife," and I press my lips to his like I did that day three years ago, kissing him aggressively and rocking back and forth on him.

He follows suit and fists his hand in my hair as he deepens the kiss.

"I love you, Riley," he breathes against my skin. "I'll never get enough of you, baby."

"I love you too." I breathe his words back at him as he strips my dress from me before lifting me just enough to shuck his swimming trunks completely off.

He settles me back down on him, his swollen trunk gliding inside my wet heat until he's filling me to the brim like he always does.

I gasp. Even after three years and having a baby, I still have trouble taking him sometimes.

He groans as he holds me close and begins to rut up into me while kissing and nipping my shoulder.

It's just like that day three years ago, only this time we're both completely naked and bared to the moonlight. It's like we're in some ethereal parallel universe to that time. Nostalgia is teasing at my senses while I'm flooded with entirely new and present sensations. It's a heady cocktail that has me edging closer and closer to that precipice that promises ecstasy.

I spear my fingers into his hair and hold on for dear life when he picks up the tempo, hitting that sweet spot inside me over and over again until I shatter.

I scream as my orgasm crashes over me. A second later, I feel his heat flooding me as he roars out his own release.

We slump against each other, holding each other close as our heartbeats return to normal.

Parker places a kiss right over my heart. "Tell me you're mine, little bird."

"I'm yours," I promise him again.

Always and forever.

THE END

Connect with Emma!

Visit Emma's website to get a FREE book you can't get anywhere else: www.authoremmabray.com.

www.ingramcontent.com/pod-product-compliance
Lightning Source LLC
Chambersburg PA
CBHW020742160726

47993CB00006B/2574